Wizard McBean And His Flying Machine

by Dennis Nolan

Prentice-Hall Inc.   Englewood Cliffs, New Jersey

Printed in the United States of America

Prentice-Hall International, Inc., London
Prentice-Hall of Australia, Pty. Ltd., North Sydney
Prentice-Hall of Canada, Ltd., Toronto
Prentice-Hall of India Private Ltd., New Delhi
Prentice-Hall of Japan, Inc., Tokyo
Prentice-Hall of Southeast Asia Pte. Ltd., Singapore

10 9 8 7 6 5 4 3 2 1

Library of Congress Cataloging in Publication Data

Nolan, Dennis.
    Wizard McBean and his flying machine.

    SUMMARY: A wizard builds a machine that flies with his head in the clouds and his feet on the ground.
    [1. Flying — Fiction] I. Title.
PZ7.N678Wi [E]   77-3472
ISBN 0-13-961607-1

There once was a Wizard McBean

Who constructed a flying machine

But up in the sky

He attracted a fly

The biggest fly he'd ever seen.

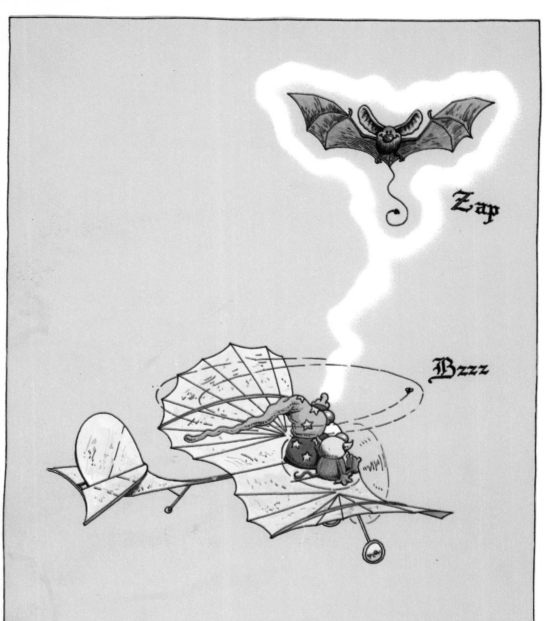

He conjured a magical plan,
A lightning bolt flew from his hand.

He needed a bat,
So he made one—like that!

And that's when his troubles began...

He had to get rid of the bat,

And he needed a dragon for that.

But the dragon roared loud;

So he zapped up a cloud,

Which slurped him, in one second flat!

Then the cloud began chasing him too

So he whipped up a wind. How it blew!

So he gave it a jolt

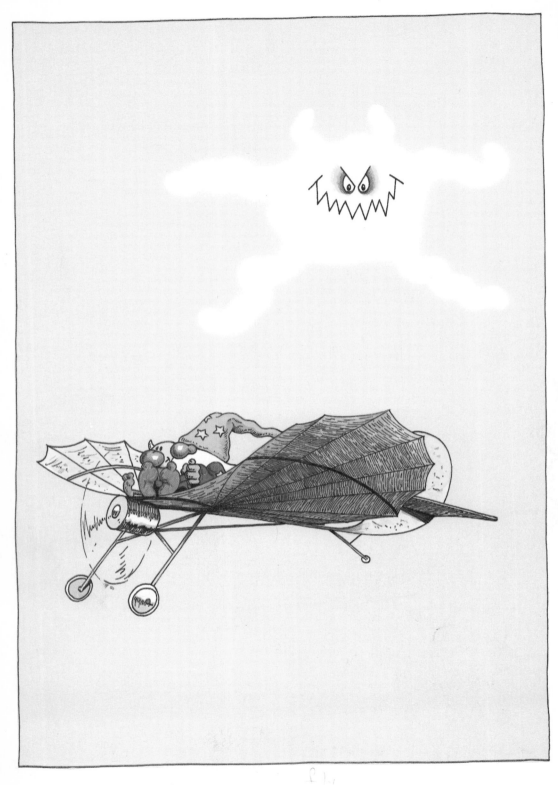

With his own lightning bolt

And believed all his troubles were through.

When Wizard McBean slammed his door
The lightning bolt struck at the floor

So he broke into rubble
The cause of his trouble

And vowed he'd go flying no more.

But McBean could not stay downhearted
Though he and his airplane had parted.

He dreamed up a car

Putt
Putt
Putt

To go near and far

Now he's right back where he started.